Dear Parents:

Congratulations! Your child is taking the first steps on an exciting journey. The destination? Independent reading!

STEP INTO READING® will help your child get there. The program offers five steps to reading success. Each step includes fun stories and colorful art or photographs. In addition to original fiction and books with favorite characters, there are Step into Reading Non-Fiction Readers, Phonics Readers and Boxed Sets, Sticker Readers, and Comic Readers—a complete literacy program with something to interest every child.

Learning to Read, Step by Step!

Ready to Read Preschool–Kindergarten
• big type and easy words • rhyme and rhythm • picture clues
For children who know the alphabet and are eager to begin reading.

Reading with Help Preschool–Grade 1
• basic vocabulary • short sentences • simple stories
For children who recognize familiar words and sound out new words with help.

Reading on Your Own Grades 1–3
• engaging characters • easy-to-follow plots • popular topics
For children who are ready to read on their own.

Reading Paragraphs Grades 2–3
• challenging vocabulary • short paragraphs • exciting stories
For newly independent readers who read simple sentences with confidence.

Ready for Chapters Grades 2–4
• chapters • longer paragraphs • full-color art
For children who want to take the plunge into chapter books but still like colorful pictures.

STEP INTO READING® is designed to give every child a successful reading experience. The grade levels are only guides; children will progress through the steps at their own speed, developing confidence in their reading.

Remember, a lifetime love of reading starts with a single step!

Copyright © 2020 Disney Enterprises, Inc. Published in the United States by Random House
Children's Books, a division of Penguin Random House LLC, 1745 Broadway, New York, NY
10019, and in Canada by Penguin Random House Canada Limited, Toronto, in conjunction with
Disney Enterprises, Inc.

Step into Reading, Random House, and the Random House colophon are registered trademarks of
Penguin Random House LLC.

Visit us on the Web!
StepIntoReading.com
rhcbooks.com

Educators and librarians, for a variety of teaching tools, visit us at RHTeachersLibrarians.com

ISBN 978-0-7364-4082-0 (trade) — ISBN 978-0-7364-8293-6 (lib. bdg.)
ISBN 978-0-7364-4083-7 (ebook)

Printed in the United States of America
10 9 8 7 6 5 4 3 2 1

Disney

FROZEN II

Olaf Loves to Read!

by John Edwards

illustrated by the Disney Storybook Art Team

Random House 🏠 New York

Anna and Olaf walk
through town.
They see the librarian,
Oddvar, at the library.

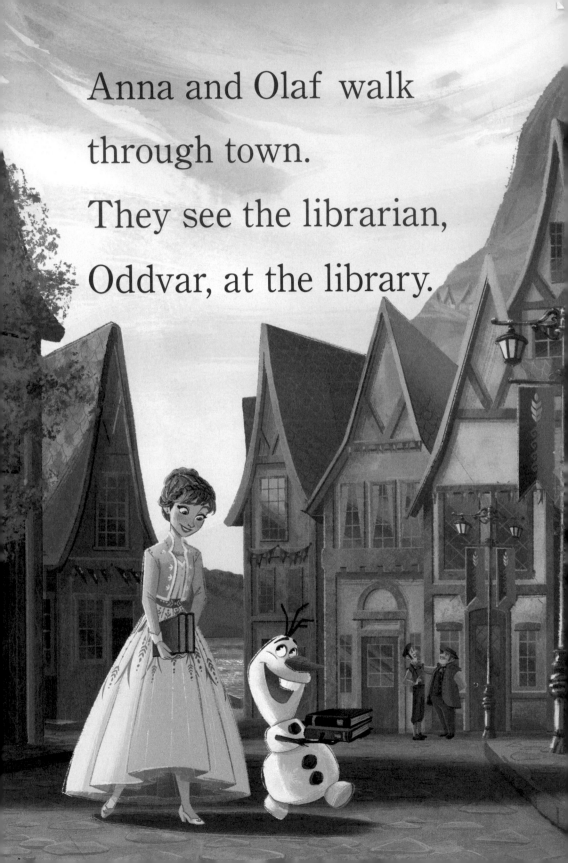

Oddvar is going
to visit his family.
There is no one
to watch the library
while he is gone.

Anna has an idea.

Olaf can be

the librarian!

Olaf agrees.

He loves to read!

Oddvar leaves.

Anna and Olaf
wave goodbye.

Anna leaves, too.

Olaf is alone
in the library.
There are so many books!

He wants to read
them all.

Olaf is having

so much fun.

Some children from
the village watch him.

Olaf makes reading fun!
The children join him
in the library.

He finds a book
for everyone.

More and more people
visit the library.
Olaf is very happy!
He gives lots of
warm hugs.

Anna returns.

She is shocked.

The library is

full of people!

Anna walks inside.
Olaf has changed
everything!

He created works of art.

He built a castle.

He even sorted books

by color!

Oddvar returns
to the library, too.
He looks around
and smiles.

Oddvar loves what
Olaf has done.
The library is now
full of people!
He gives the snowman
a warm hug.

Oddvar asks Olaf to keep
working at the library.

The snowman is thrilled!

His friends come to help.

The whole town
agrees that Olaf
is a great librarian!